APR 1 0

THE SECRETS OF DROON

Sorcerer

by Tony Abbott

Illustrated by David Merrell

Cover illustration by Tim Jessell

A
LITTLE APPLE
PAPERBACK

SCHOLASTIC INC.
New York Toronto London Auckland Sydney
Mexico City New Delhi Hong Kong Buenos Aires

For my family,
near, far, everywhere

For more information about the continuing saga of Droon,
please visit Tony Abbott's website at
www.tonyabbottbooks.com

ISBN 0-439-67178-7

12 11 10 9 8 7 6 5 4 3 2   6 7 8 9 10 11/0

Printed in the U.S.A.
First printing, October 2006

Contents

One

To the Ends of the Earth

Call me Sparr. I am a sorcerer. An enchanter. A conjuror. Dark magic sings in my veins. My powers are nearly limitless. Spells, charms, curses — I've used them all to achieve my goals.

My enemies call me "pure evil."

Still, I didn't start out that way, did I?

I like to think I was a friendly little child, very much like you. I loved to run and play and climb and jump. I even had a cute puppy who followed me everywhere.

What could make me turn so bad? Why do I use dark powers? Most important, how did I really become *Lord Sparr*?

Hold on tight, my friend, and I'll tell you. It's a bumpy ride. A thrilling adventure. There are some funny parts. Perhaps you'll even shed a tear or two.

Most of all, look closely and you'll see . . . everything. Let's begin with this morning. Look there. There. In the sky!

Whoosh-shoosh! Rough winds stung my weathered face. Waves crashed and spat icy water into my piercing eyes. Arrows, flaming and deadly, whizzed swiftly past my head.

"Faster!" I cried. "Into the clouds! Fly!"

I dug in my heels and — *zzzt-zzzt-whoooosh!* — the great shiny wings of my Golden Wasp blurred with speed. Up we swept over the stormy waves.

"Excuse me, but they're catching up, you know," grumbled a voice at my shoulder. "I can smell their bad breath."

That was Kem, my two-headed pet dog. Nearly as old as me, Kem had been my companion almost from the beginning. We had been through a lot together.

We were about to go through more.

Fwing—clang! A flaming stinger struck the Wasp's tail and shot off into the clouds.

Sneaking a look behind me, I spied a sky nearly black with tangled swarms of fiery wingsnakes. The fearsome, four-winged moon dragon called Gethwing led them through the air.

Down below, slicing across the dark

waves of the Serpent Sea in his ship, was the twin-horned, three-eyed beast ruler himself, Emperor Ko. Behind him swam a vast force of beasts.

They were all after me.

"You shall never escape me and my army, you traitor!" the emperor's thunderous voice boomed.

"Unless my wingsnakes and I destroy you first!" cried Gethwing.

Kem held on more tightly. "Hmm. You and me against a million bad guys. Nice odds. Too bad we don't have many friends."

"Many friends?" I snorted. "Try *any* friends!" In the far distance, I saw the royal fleet of King Zello and Queen Relna, sailing away across the dark seas. I had battled them and their daughter, Keeah, for many years. I'd fought the master wizard Galen and the children from the Upper World—Eric

Hinkle, Julie Rubin, and Neal Kroger — for a long time, too. None of them were about to help me.

My thoughts and feelings stormed inside me as I watched the fleet fade into the distance. For a time — a brief time — I had been a boy again and had become their good friend.

I would lie if I said that meant nothing.

But while they were leaving, my enemies were gaining on me, closing in faster, faster.

"Sparr, I will find you!" shouted Ko. "I will stop you! I will have my Coiled Viper back!"

Ah, yes, the Coiled Viper.

Perhaps the most dangerous of my Three Powers, the Viper was a large gold crown in the shape of a snake twined upon itself.

I had used the Viper to bring Ko back

from his four-century sleep. It was the Viper that gave him his awesome power. It was the Viper that transformed me from a sorcerer into the ten-year-old boy who became the children's friend. And it was the Viper that finally turned me back into my bad old self again.

Right now, the magical crown was hooked safely on my belt.

"I'd get rid of that thing," yelled Kem. "Maybe Ko will even let us go. Maybe?"

I grimaced at the dog. We both knew that wasn't true. I had betrayed Ko by stealing the Viper from him. Now he would pursue me to the ends of the earth.

And the ends of the earth, it seemed, was just where we were going.

"Faster, Wasp!" I cried. "And take a left!"

Whoosh! We made a vast loop away from the sea, soared over a mountaintop, then dived out of the clouds and over the rugged land below. In the distance lay the hollow of a deep valley.

Ah! I thought. *The Valley of Pits!*

The ruins of a great old palace lay almost hidden under the sands of the valley. They were the remains of Ko's old empire of Goll. Ko needed the Viper to help him bring his dark empire back.

"Look there," said Kem, craning his necks as we swept over the ruins. "The Ninns. They're waiting for you to return to them."

I glanced down. Camped out in an oasis among the palace ruins was a small troop of plump red-faced warriors called Ninns. The Ninns are a tribe that goes back to the very beginning of Goll.

"Never mind them," I said, as we headed out to sea again. "I have the Skorth now."

Kem snorted. "Oh, yeah. Fun guys, the Skorth. Always a riot."

The Warriors of the Skorth were not

fun. They were a ruthless race of soulless skeleton soldiers. Right now they sailed below us in their fleet of ghostly ships. Nearly unconquerable, they had agreed to help me fight Ko. Their numbers were in the thousands.

I swept low and hailed them. "Skorth! Turn your ships. Stop Ko from coming any farther until I escape!"

The ghost ships slowed, turned, and formed an unwavering wall against Ko's advancing serpents. A fierce battle began.

This didn't stop Gethwing, however. The moon dragon's flock of wingsnakes banked suddenly behind us and swooped like a tattered, windblown scarf across the air.

"Faster, Wasp!" I cried.

My buzzing creature redoubled its speed while I swung around, flicked my fingers, and sent off several powerful blasts at our pursuers.

Blam-blam-blam! The wingsnakes arched up to avoid my blasts, then responded with an attack of flaming stingers.

"Dive, quickly!" I yelled.

The Wasp spun violently out of the way, and my hand clutched instinctively at my cloak pocket. When we righted again, I pulled out a little stone and held it tight in my fist.

The stone was black and sprinkled with silver ore in some places, veined with blue and violet streaks in others.

Earlier that morning, as I changed back into my adult form, Eric Hinkle had risked his own life to give me the stone.

"The young wizard gave me this," I said to Kem.

"And I wish it were a life preserver," my

dog replied, glancing back over his shoulder with one head. "Gethwing's coming even faster now —"

"My history of four hundred years of evil has nearly erased the image of this stone from my mind, and yet . . . I have seen it before, haven't I? Once, long ago, when I was young . . ."

"Try thinking about right now!" cried Kem. "There's a storm dead ahead! Fly north! Or south! Or anywhere else — Sparr!"

I stared into a broadening funnel of black wind swirling up from the sea not five miles in front of us. It grew more monstrous by the second. Grinning to myself, I kicked the Wasp for more speed. "Yes, yes, faster!"

"Sparr, don't even think about it —"

"Kem, don't be such a puppy!" I said. "If we can fly through the storm, perhaps we can lose our enemies!"

"*If? Perhaps?*" yelped Kem. "Lose our *lives*, you mean! Sparr, you're *not* going to fly into that storm. You absolutely are not —"

"And — here — we — go!"

Digging the Wasp sharply with my heels, I aimed us toward the storm and — *whoom!* — we crashed straight into its wall of black wind. The Wasp faltered. We began to fall.

"Uh-oh," I said. "Wrong move —"

Howling a terrifying laugh, Gethwing dived toward us, his wingsnakes close behind.

"Get us out of here!" I cried. But the storm winds drew us right to them, battering us from every direction. The Wasp couldn't pull away. All of a sudden, a bolt of silver light sliced through the storm and cut across the air in front of us.

"Veer away, Wasp!" I yelled, yanking up on the golden reins. "Fly!" The buzzing beast tried to pull away from the bolt of light but could not. The light descended over us like a falling sword.

"Ahh!" I screamed as the bolt struck my forehead, knocking me from the Wasp's back.

I fell . . . fell . . . fell . . . toward the heaving black sea. Kem plummeted into the water first. I dropped right behind him. The sea was as hard as iron when I struck its surface.

The Viper broke off my belt.

I tried to reach it but couldn't. The cold water hissed and boiled around it, and the blazing golden crown vanished into a spinning funnel of darkness. It was gone.

Flailing in the freezing water, I reached for Kem, but he fell deeper and deeper below me, and everything turned as black as night.

My head burned. My body twisted in

pain, then went limp. My lungs filled with icy water.

I sank.

Darkness closed over me.

I drowned.

Two

A Man and His Dog

Almost.

My lungs burned like fire. I wanted air, but when I gasped for it, my lips burst apart and all that poured into my mouth was the icy black water of the Serpent Sea.

No, no! I thought. *Is this how it ends?*

All of a sudden — *splash! slursh! slud-d-d!* — I was out of the water, being dragged facedown on dry land.

"S-s-s-stop!" I gagged, spitting water and sand from my mouth. "I'm choking —"

"Should I stop saving you, then?" grumbled a familiar voice. "Fine."

Kem let go of my feet, and they hit the ground. *Thunk. Thunk.* I rolled over and sat up, gulping air as if trying to swallow the sky.

My eyes stung with foul seawater. I rubbed them for what seemed like forever. When I finally opened them, I was nearly blinded by a bright white light.

Sunlight?

Sunlight!

Kem slumped down next to me, panting. "You're heavy."

"But alive," I replied.

"Mmm, barely."

We rested in silence for a few minutes, trying to get our bearings. A beach of soft silver sand spread out all around us. The sun was bright overhead, but a giant wall of spinning black wind surrounded the land in every direction like a cloak.

A thick jungle of strange, gnarly plants made up most of the island beyond the beach. The odd tendrils looked like the roots of some upside-down tree, pointed and stark against the blue sky, yet beautiful in their own way. The whole jungle coiled up in an ever-twisting mass until it was lost in a fog-shrouded summit.

"How odd," I said.

"Odd, is it?" said Kem, following my gaze. "You mean landing on a deserted island paradise smack in the middle of a hurricane? I think it's our lucky day."

I wobbled to my feet and shook the sand from my cloak. My hands were clenched in fists. Only when I went to open them did I realize that I was holding something. Miraculously, after my fall and near drowning, the stone had not fallen out of my hand.

"So . . . what is this place?" I wondered, carefully dropping the stone into my cloak pocket.

"Well," said Kem, shaking the water from his fur and spraying me, "judging by the sky full of no wingsnakes and the sea full of no Ko, I'd say we're somewhere safe. For now."

I smiled. "You see, my furry friend, my plan did work. We *are* safe. And warm! And drying by the minute. It's almost too good to be —" I gasped. "Kem! This isn't . . . I mean . . . we're not . . . *dead* . . . are we?"

I should say that Kem usually spoke with his right head, but grumbled with both.

He grumbled with both heads now. "Dead? Probably not. When you die, there's supposed to be food everywhere. At least for dogs, there is. I don't see any food."

Trying to walk, I found that I ached all over. My forehead stung. When I put my hand up to it, I pulled it away with a cry. "Oww — I must have hit my head!"

"Ooh, an improvement," Kem grumbled.

I glared at the dog. "Do you speak only to torment me?"

He looked thoughtful for a moment, then shook both heads. "No. That's just a bonus. Come on. Let's snoop around. Ever since I mentioned food, it's all I can think about."

I breathed in the warm air. "Lead the way."

We started walking down the beach. The island, as it turned out, was not very big. It took no longer than an hour to walk around the entire shore and back to where we started.

The island bore a crescent shape, like a quarter moon. Long arms of land curved out on either end to a pair of points, creating a natural bay between them.

What is this place? I wondered. *Are we really saved? Was it simply luck that brought us here? Or was it something else?*

"Kem, as far as I know, there aren't any islands this far east in the Serpent Sea. And this storm? Isn't it strange how it keeps our enemies away?"

"Our enemies?" he said. "*Your* enemies."

"Yet keeps the island itself basking in the warmth of the morning sun?"

"'Basking in the warmth of the morning sun,'" he repeated dryly. "What have I told you about your words? You're an evil sorcerer, Sparr, not a poet."

No, not a poet. And yet as we trod the silvery sands, I felt . . . different. I was a sorcerer, feared and hated across Droon for four hundred years. But not two days before,

I had been a boy whom Galen, Max, and the children were beginning to trust.

To *trust*!

"Kem?" I said. "Having been a boy again has left me with odd thoughts. Misty memories of the long past. Images. Feelings. Things are different, Kem. I think *I* am different."

The dog stopped sniffing, sighed, sat, and raised his heads to me. "Different, are you? All right. Here's a test. You say the first thing that pops into your head. Ready? An ugly moon dragon comes up to you. What do you do?"

I didn't even think about it. "Blast him with sparks!"

"Very good. But suppose he's got a steaming gizzleberry pie?"

"I'd still blast him. The pie is probably poisoned."

"Of course. Now suppose a little spider troll charges at you with a very big knife?"

"I look for a very big fork and spoon and join him for supper?"

The dog stared at me with a frown. "Well. That's not very evil, is it? Maybe you really *are* different — holy smoke, look at that!"

Turning, I saw a line of footprints in the sand. The prints were shallow but wide and short. They wove along the shore for a distance, then vanished into the jungle.

"Sparr, this deserted island is not so deserted," said Kem. "Someone else is here."

"But not a large person, if it is a person at all," I said. "Let's be careful. I fear danger may lurk among the oddly twisting roots and vines of this jungle."

The dog snorted. "'Danger may lurk,'" he said. "You and your words. Come on."

Together we pressed into the thick

jumble of growth, and almost at once I began to hear sounds jingling in the branches, strange musical clatterings like chimes in the wind.

Wait. Chimes in the wind?

I closed my eyes. *Do I remember something about chimes? What was it?*

"Kem —"

"Soup!" he said suddenly. "I smell soup!"

I crept up next to him. Bending to his level, I sniffed. "It does smell like soup. Good nose . . . noses."

"Yeah, well, smells are my thing."

Easing quietly through the undergrowth, we saw a small stack of logs set between two stout trees. At first, I thought it was simply a pile of wood. But as we got closer, I saw a faint coil of smoke rising from it. A door was cleverly hidden under the vines and roots clinging to the logs.

Putting my finger to my lips, I set my

hand on the latch and lifted it. The door opened a crack. A fog of soupy smells wafted out.

"Ohhhh!" Kem gasped softly. "Lunch!"

When the steam cleared, we peeked in to see someone moving around inside a tiny room. It was a short blue-skinned creature with a large head and wiry body.

"A troll!" I whispered. "An island troll!"

Bushy blue whiskers nearly hid a great bulbous nose. The troll was very old, with wrinkles all over his face and hands nearly purple with age. But he was very active! Unaware of us, the troll sprang about the tiny room, pulling bottles down from a high shelf, then spinning around and spooning cups of this and that from barrels on the floor.

All these ingredients went into a giant pot that bubbled over a fire. Standing on a

stool and stirring the pot was a tiny green monkey.

Catching sight of me, the monkey jumped. "Eeep!"

Without turning from his pot, the troll said, "Hold on, hold on, friends! The soup's not quite ready!"

The monkey *eeep*ed again. When the troll glanced over his shoulder, he gasped. "Oh! You aren't my friends! That is, I don't mean that you are my *enemies*. It's just that, excuse me — we haven't been properly introduced!" He bowed politely and said, "I am Beffo, King of the Island Trolls! Well, really, the only island troll at the moment. Who are you?"

I blinked at the blue face, frowned, and cleared my throat. "I do understand we're miles from everywhere, little person, but are you saying you don't know who I am?"

The troll beamed suddenly. "Santa?"

I frowned. "No, no. Think dark. Think evil. Then multiply it! I'm worse!"

"Much worse!" added Kem. "I've seen him in action. I know. He does terrible stuff."

The troll gasped at Kem. "Did your dog just say something? It sounded almost like . . . words!"

Kem grumbled. "Oh, let him hear me, Sparr. It's so boring talking only to you."

I chuckled, then snapped my fingers with a brief whisper. When Kem spoke this time, repeating what he had first said, the troll understood every word.

Beffo's eyes went wide. "Well, you're certainly both very strange. And magical! Perhaps if I offer you soup you won't put a spell on us? Besides, with this storm, there's no getting off the island until nightfall, so you might as well share our meal with us!"

I narrowed my eyes at the troll. "How do you know how long the storm will last?"

He took the ladle from the monkey and stirred his giant pot so vigorously that it hissed. "I study the clouds, you know. That's my thing. So, now, tell me. What *is* your name?"

"Lord Sparr," I said. "Sorcerer! Magician!"

"Magician!" he yelped. "I love magic! In fact, I like to imagine I'm a great and powerful wizard who can change shape and travel around in time! But, hee-hee, I'm simply a troll!"

At that moment, the doors creaked open and four more green monkeys trotted in. They chirped and chattered to one another when they saw Kem and me, then settled by the fire next to Beffo.

"You know," I said, observing the monkeys closely, "if we weren't almost halfway across the world, I'd say your friends are monkeys from the Bangledorn Forest."

Beffo chuckled knowingly as he stirred. "The Bangledorn Forest is *exactly* halfway across the world, in fact —"

A sudden wind moved over the jungle outside and, as before, it sang with the sound of chimes. What caused me to clutch the stone in my pocket then, I cannot say. But as I did, the troll's fire leaped up around the pot, licking its sides with tongues of gold.

Whether the flames suddenly affected me, or I was influencing them, or it was the bump on my head, or the strange and beautiful island itself, I do not know. But I could not take my eyes from the fire. And it seemed to me that the tighter I held that black stone, the more I began to see shapes appearing among the hearth's dancing wisps of flame.

At once, I began to remember things from when I was a boy. I was overcome with recollections of times gone by. A long-forgotten story surfaced from the depths of my memory. My eyes stung, and I closed them.

"What is it?" said the troll, sipping from his ladle, then continuing to stir.

"You want to travel in time, old fellow? Well, I'll take you back. I'm beginning to remember something . . . about myself. . . ."

"Oh, wonderful," snorted Kem. "This is all he needs. An audience to listen to him talk about himself. You'll never stop him now."

The more the flames flitted up the sides of the pot, the more I seemed to see a figure. No . . . two figures. They were running. . . .

"Excuse me, Sparr?" said Kem, waving a paw in front of me. "You still here?"

"Behold!" I said, raising my hands to the fire. "The veil of the past is drawn aside!

I see a boy four centuries ago. He is running. With" —I turned to Kem — "his dog!"

"Wait!" cried Beffo. He whirled around, grabbed several pillows from the corner of the hut, and stuffed them behind his back.

"Go ahead, then," he said. "I'll stir the pot. You stir your memory. Speak . . . speak . . ."

As if the little troll's words were a command, I did stir my memory.

The fire crackled and sparks spat up to the ceiling. I stared into the coiling flames, and I was no longer in the troll's tiny hut. I was running down a narrow stone passage. My puppy, Kem, was scampering at my heels.

"It is four hundred years ago, on one of my last days . . . without . . . these!"

I stroked the serpent fins behind my ears.

An instant later, I was there.

Three

The Forbidden Room

"Kem, hurry!" I whispered, glancing back into the dim passage behind us.

It was four centuries ago in Emperor Ko's palace in the Valley of Pits, at the very center of the ancient Empire of Goll.

"I hear footsteps," I hissed. "We're being followed. We can't fail on our mission. Be quick about it!"

"I'm being quick!" said Kem, galloping at my heels, one head watching over his shoulder. "But there really isn't any mission."

"If I say we're on a mission, we're on one! Now, *shhh*!" I skittered breathlessly down a long hallway, screeched to a halt at the corner, and peeked around. "Wait — this courtyard again? I can't believe this crazy palace. Kem, we're back where we started!"

My little friend whimpered, "You mean your 'mission' to get away from Old Four Wings has led us right back to him?"

"Sorry," I said.

Old Four Wings was the dreaded moon dragon, Gethwing. And our mission was to skip my morning magic lesson.

Gethwing was my teacher, and he was mad at me. While trying to peel a banana using just my thoughts, I had accidentally melted his favorite sword and broken a chair, a vase, two bottles, and his war helmet.

I also set fire to his tail. And his breakfast.

I knew he didn't expect me to have such power. I also knew he'd take total revenge on me today with some impossible task.

As the footsteps grew closer behind us, the sudden scent of moon dragon wafted across the opening to the courtyard.

"Gethwing's in his room . . . above us," whispered Kem. "We'll never cross the yard without him spotting us. We're trapped."

"Oh?" I said with a grin. "Did you forget my latest charm? The Foggy Cloud of Mist?"

Kem shook his heads nervously. "I thought it was the Misty Cloud of Fog. And it doesn't work, anyway, does it? Besides, Gethwing doesn't like you using your own magic —"

"He won't see us!" I said. "Come on."

While Kem muttered to himself, I spoke the charm I had made up. *"Selat hemp na-na fo."*

Hoooo! A haze of air surrounded us, hiding us from each other and from everyone else.

"Here we go," I said. "Wish us luck!"

He squeaked. "Why do we need luck?"

"I haven't been able to figure out how to keep the charm going, so it might fade a bit early," I said. "No big deal. Just be quick. And quiet!"

My heart nearly burst with excitement as we crept into the courtyard. It was stark and spare, but shafts of green light from the torches lining the upper terraces danced across the stones. They made a wild pattern in front of my feet.

Suddenly, the shadow of a giant wing fell over the mist. We froze where we stood and looked up. The moon dragon was pacing the terrace outside his chamber. Every few moments, he paused and stared down.

Kem trembled, trying to hide under me. "Some mission. Right under Gethwing's snout. He'll see us for sure!"

The dragon began pacing again, and I realized that not only did he not see us, he wasn't looking for us, either. Then he whispered something, and I heard someone reply.

It was the voice of a young girl.

"Kem, he's not alone up there!" I said.

As I watched, a girl with long dark hair and a strange wild look in her eyes came forward. She spoke as if she were in some kind of trance. I couldn't make out all her words.

"... boy ... future ... secret stone ... lord ... home ..."

I nudged Kem. "Secret stone? What

stone? What is Gethwing up to? Lord? Home? Who is that girl? I've never seen her before."

"All very good questions," he said, "but can we please get out of here? Please?"

Glancing both ways, Kem and I sprinted across the open space, careful to stay under the mist. I looked back, but Gethwing had already retreated into his chamber. The girl was gone.

It was a good thing, because a moment later — *fzzzz!* — the Cloudy Fog of Mist vanished. We were in plain sight again.

Thomp! Thomp!

"I hear guards!" Kem winced. "You and your missions. Hide!"

"I wish we *were* on a real mission!" I said as we dashed into the shadows. "I had a dream that I was in battle —"

Making my way forward in the darkness, my hands discovered a door. It was barred shut. Without thinking, I flicked my finger at the door and — *clink-clank!* — the bars fell away.

"Whoa!" I whispered. "That's new!"

I pushed. The door creaked open.

"But, Master, wait!" Kem grumbled. "Not this room. It's forbidden —"

Too late. A troop of hustling guards stormed through the passage, and Kem and I tumbled into the dim room. Closing the door behind us, we flattened against the wall and held our breath. In the near silence of the room, I heard the soft jangle of chimes.

Chimes!

Kem kept his ears to the door. "They're gone. The hall is clear now. Let's go." When I didn't move, Kem nudged my knees with one head and tugged my cloak with the other. "Sparr! Out —"

But I was frozen where I stood.

We were alone in a chamber filled with

magnificent furniture, golden and bejeweled. In its center stood a large empty bed covered in tapestries. It all shone dimly from a single torch flickering on the wall near the ceiling.

"Sparr, let's go. Please!" Kem urged.

"Kem, no." I pushed him away. The whole back wall behind the empty bed was painted to look like the room itself. Only in the wall painting, the bed was not empty.

In it lay the figure of a dead woman.

Her face was as still and white as the robe she wore. Circling her head was a crown shimmering with its own silver glow. It was Zara, the Queen of Light. It was my mother.

I breathed deeply, feeling suddenly weak, as if I wanted to cry. "Mother . . ."

At my word, the torch's flame seemed to leap up and fall back.

Emperor Ko was also in the picture.

Even painted, he was a frightening figure, with his enormous bull head and his twin horns smoldering. His three red eyes glared down at the lifeless form of my mother.

"Time to go," Kem murmured. "I hear more guards coming. This time, they might find us!"

With a single step, I was at the empty bed. I touched its sunken pillow.

"Kem, my mother died in this room," I said.

"I know," he murmured, softening a little. "I was here, remember?"

I squeezed my eyes shut tightly.

Being in her room, I felt my mother's absence like a fresh wound. Yet I also felt closer to her than I had in a very long time.

Another troop of guards rushed down the passages outside the chamber, and Kem tugged on my cloak again.

"Wipe your face, Sparr," he said.

"What's done is done. Queen Zara . . . your mother . . . is not here anymore. She is —"

"Where is she, Kem?" I snapped. "Where? If she's . . . dead, where is her tomb? Why can't I visit her? See her?"

A third rush of heavy feet thundered down the hall, more quickly this time. Then an unearthly wail shrieked through the palace, echoing in every passage.

"The arena," said Kem. "Ko is calling everyone to the arena. Sparr, something's really happening. Forget skipping your lesson. This is big. We have to go, too —"

He pulled me from my mother's room and into the hall, where we were nearly run over by a troop of lion-shaped beasts carrying four-bladed spears.

"To the arena!" the lion's leader announced. "We are going to war!" They tore off again through the passage toward the great stadium, pulling us along with them.

The farther I moved from my mother's room, the more thoughts of her faded like my own faulty charm. With each step, my sorrow seemed to drain away and be replaced by anger and revenge. My blood began to boil.

"The Destroyer!" I growled, my heart beating like a gong. "For years now, Ko has told me that my mother was poisoned by someone called the Destroyer. If there is war, maybe I can go on a real mission. Maybe I'll find this Destroyer, whoever he is. I have magic. I'll fight him. I'll have my revenge!"

"Oh, no more missions!" Kem sighed.

Five minutes later, we emerged from the palace into a vast outdoor stadium. A large iron throne sat nearby. Ko himself stood in front of it. Gethwing was by his side, along with a ferocious-looking woolly beast that was armed all over with plates of thick metal.

The arena's stands were already filled with thousands upon thousands of cheering beasts.

"Silence!" boomed the emperor, and the arena went quiet. He scanned the crowd. "Sparr, my boy. I see you. Come. Join me!"

I trembled, but dared not — could not — disobey.

As we made our way to the throne, Kem whimpered, "I don't like the way Ko looks at me. As if I'm . . ."

"A tiny puppy?" I said.

"A great big snack!" he said with a gulp.

I knew what he meant. My heart shivered just thinking about the emperor's fiery gaze. And yet as I approached Ko, I felt drawn to his awesome power.

Ko was the great leader of millions of beasts across half of Droon. He wanted to extend his empire of Goll across the rest of the world, too. Ko even called me the Prince of Goll.

Rising to the throne, I bowed before the emperor. He was dressed from head to foot in black armor, all spiked and bladed. He turned to the woolly beast. "Tell us what you saw!"

The beast bowed, unrolled a scroll, and began to read from it. "The northern wall of Goll was breached in the dead of night. The enemy has sailed into the port of Nerona. Our empire is under attack!"

The crowd began to stomp and shout.

"There is more!" shouted the beast. "The Destroyer is with them. He commands the enemy fleet!"

I nearly exploded. *The Destroyer? The person who killed my mother?*

"War!" shouted the beasts in the arena.

Ko raised his four hands high, his horns spraying fire ten feet into the air. "There shall be war! Gethwing, my commander?"

The emperor's lieutenant stepped forward.

If I was in awe of Ko, I distrusted Gethwing. From the moment he became my tutor, I knew he didn't really like me. I was Zara's son. I might develop my own great powers. He knew that sooner or later I could challenge him. I think I knew it, too.

The arena went silent when the moon dragon spoke. "Beasts, we are at war, and we shall crush the attackers with our invincible army," he said calmly, his eyes flicking toward me. "But there is something to try first, before an all-out attack. A . . . mission. A *secret* mission. Before dawn tomorrow, we can sink the enemy fleet to the bottom of Nerona's bay. The Destroyer can be defeated —"

Almost despite my fear, I jumped up.

"Ko, send me! Send me! Let me help destroy the enemy fleet! Let me face this Destroyer, killer of my mother!"

A long moment of silence followed. My words hung in the air.

Gethwing leaned over to Ko and whispered in his ear. A smile moved across the emperor's face.

"Perhaps it may take a boy, after all, to slip through the enemy's defenses and stop the Destroyer. Your anger will drive you to victory. So, my young Prince of Goll, let this be your first true mission!"

"Yes!" I cried, my heart soaring. "Emperor, you won't be sorry!"

Ko looked at me with his three eyes, then reached behind his throne. "I give you two weapons," he said. "With this sword you will battle the Destroyer. This helmet will protect you, help you see in the dark, and breathe and speak underwater. Wear it always when you are out of my sight. In it, you shall hear my words and see through my eyes."

The sword was curved and had a fine handle encrusted with jewels and red stones. The helmet was black and shaped like Ko's own bull head, a pair of horns arching from the top.

"This mission is the first that shall take you beyond the limits of my palace," he said. "I hope it will not be the last."

My heart swelled as I reached to take the weapons. "Thank you."

"A third weapon is needed, too!" said Gethwing. From nowhere, he produced a dull green orb and handed it to me. It was heavy.

"Place the orb inside the Destroyer's

ship," the moon dragon said. "When you spin it, you have five minutes to leave before it explodes."

Ko placed his massive hands on my little shoulders. "Remember, do not remove my helmet, for it will keep you safe. Return in victory, and you shall truly be my Prince of Goll!"

The whole arena of beasts erupted in a cheer. "Hail, Prince of Goll!"

Ko hushed the crowd. "I go now to the Iron Gate to raise the Seven Giants. Together we'll strike the enemy and crush them at Nerona!"

The emperor stormed from the arena amid the cheers from thousands of bellowing beasts.

I stood there, trembling to think about what I had agreed to do. Kem trembled, too.

Gethwing stepped over to me, his eyes

burning into mine. "I can tell that you have been in your mother's chamber. It is not wise to visit that room. Think not of the past, Sparr. That time is over."

Kem grumbled under his breath.

"But never mind!" the dragon said brightly. "Guards, the boy will need tools to enter the Destroyer's ship. Take him to the armory. He and the dog must be outfitted for their mission!"

Before I knew it, Gethwing was gone, and Kem and I were being hurried through the passages of the palace.

"Uh, guards?" Kem asked. "Is there such a thing as puppy armor? Something with two helmets in matching colors, maybe?"

Gethwing's guards did not answer. They hurried on.

Four

Pretty in Pink

Errrr!

The moment the palace gates squealed open, I rushed out, my heart leaping as high as the horns of my helmet.

Looking out through the helmet's eye-holes, I needed no torchlight to see the two long rows of armored beasts on either side of a road curving away from the Valley of Pits.

"Come, our Prince of Goll!" called

Gethwing. "March with me at the army's head!"

"Amazing!" I whispered. "Kem, come on."

"I'm with you," he said.

When we reached the front of the troops, Gethwing raised his arm toward the distance and let it fall. The ground thundered as the army began its long march, and Kem and I rushed along in the excitement of our adventurous mission —

"Stop!" said Kem. He was peering eagerly over the top of Beffo's bubbling pot.

I frowned at the dog. "What is it?"

"Your words!" Kem said. "Maybe you 'rushed along in the excitement of our adventurous mission,' but I didn't! I sort of clanked and clunked. My armor was made of spare parts and pinched like crazy, you know. Your official Junior Ko helmet wasn't all that spiffy, either. Silly horns, bull face, weird red eyeholes. It was a miracle you could see at all!"

I stared into the fire, and the images moved again among the flames. "You're right, Kem. You're right . . . left . . . right . . . left . . ."

✷

We marched over the black earth, a nearly unending river of warriors, moving steadily to the north to save our empire from the Destroyer.

What it was, I couldn't say then, but the beasts had never seemed so valiant as when I beheld them through the red visor of the helmet Ko had given me.

Hours came and hours went until, near dawn, the great army began to slow. One of the troop leaders clambered up the side of a hill and peered over the top.

"Ninns!" he whispered. He waved for Gethwing to follow.

"Come, boy," said the dragon. "And learn."

Together, Kem and I scrambled after Gethwing to the top of the hill. Sure enough, a camp of red war tents was nestled in a small valley below. An armed troop of plump, red-faced warriors was milling around. I had heard about the Ninn tribes. They were scattered across Droon, but Ko was uniting them under his power.

"Ninns are a strange lot," said the dragon. "I don't trust them. They have their own little villages, but they are mostly loyal to Ko. Let's see if they know anything."

We crept down the hill to the Ninn camp.

"Nerona lies ready for war," said the largest of the red warriors when Gethwing questioned him. "Look." He turned and we all followed his gaze through a pass in the hills.

A dark city was perched on an inlet of the northern sea. Cramped streets, eerie bridges, and frightening coiled towers were surrounded by a wall whose jagged points ran along the entire length of the city.

"I saw this place on a map in Ko's war room once," said Kem, peering through the eyeholes of his helmets. "Nerona is the Droon city closest to Goll."

"Ugly and scary," I murmured.

"It has been so forever," said the dragon.

"And look. Thirty warships have come," the Ninn commander added. "The *droomar* are massing to attack us again."

I scanned the shadowed bay below. What I saw were misshapen vessels, each with a fearsome face on its bow. From each deck rose a single black sail. A pair of ragged iron blades swept up from the pointed stern of each ship.

I had heard about the *droomar* — or rather, *overheard* about them — while sneaking around Ko's palace. The strange little race was ancient, mysterious, and knew very powerful magic.

As I stared at the ships, I heard Ko's gravelly voice whispering inside my helmet.

The people who built those ships, who built the city of Nerona, helped the Destroyer poison your mother, my young princeling. They showed the poor queen no mercy. The fiends!

Anger rose in me once more.

"The largest, blackest vessel in the bay is the flagship of the Destroyer," said Gethwing. "Do not forget the purpose of your mission." Turning to the Ninns, he added, "You warriors know the terrain here. Bring the boy secretly down to the port. Help in whatever way you can. My army and I shall await your signal from our position in the hills. When Emperor Ko has raised the Seven Giants, we shall combine to destroy the port and march on the *droomar* hideouts. Now, go!"

I tightened my armor as best I could, then Kem and I followed a little band of Ninns carefully down the inside of the valley. We moved quietly past the campfires of the *droomar* and into the dark city.

As quiet as we were, my heart thundered, and my brain stormed with Ko's words. I was nervous and afraid, but most of all I could not wait to confront the Destroyer.

"Kem," I whispered, my voice trembling, "I'll fight him. I'll make him taste my sorrow."

The dog looked up at me and whimpered. "Please, no poetry. And don't talk about eating at a time like this. I'm really scared!"

Through the narrow streets of Nerona we went. Soon I heard the sound of waves lapping against wooden hulls. A few moments more and Kem and I were in sight of the ships. Their great hulls sat heavy in the black water.

"Prince of Goll," said the Ninn commander, bowing as he drew away, "we will try to help you as best we can."

"Too bad you won't be there with us," muttered Kem.

Kem and I managed to slip past everyone and quietly enter the water. After a few quick strokes we found ourselves under the hull of the Destroyer's ship.

I spoke through the speaking tube of my helmet. "Kem, we don't have much time for this. It's get inside, plant the green orb, and get out as soon as possible."

"Or sooner!" he said. "Hurry!"

From my cloak, I pulled a small drill I was given in the palace armory. I jammed it into the hull just above the waterline and began to turn. Minutes later, I had pierced the hull. Drilling three more holes, then connecting them with a handsaw, I made a hole large enough for Kem and me to squeeze through.

I was stunned at the ship's cargo hold. It was filled from floor to ceiling with ugly weapons, piles of explosives, and giant, many-barreled guns.

"Terrible!" said Kem. "It looks like the Destroyer wants to be true to his name!"

In my ears, I could hear Ko's voice. *To the master engine room. Go now!*

"All right, Kem. Let's do it."

But no sooner had we stepped into the passage than our way was blocked by a large man — an enormous man! — dressed from head to foot in a frightening suit of armor. A tattered cloak as black as oil hung from his shoulders to the floor.

"The Destroyer!" I gasped.

"Me?" said the giant. "I don't think so!"

I reached to my side, and the sword Ko had given me flashed up in my hand. Its curved blade shone like a crescent moon. "Perish, you murderous fiend!"

"Again, I don't think so," he said. "Do you think maybe we should talk about this? For instance, who are you?"

Ignoring him, I leaped with my sword raised high. Jumping back, he drew a sword twice as long as my own. It had five blades! They all whirled in different directions and gave off sizzling sparks.

In seconds, we were battling for our lives!

Glonk! Flang! Boomf!

I tried my best, carving all sorts of slices

and cuts into the air, but the knight quickly overpowered me. He was so huge! Finally, he thrust at me with his sword and the green orb fell from my hand. It spun on the floor and began to smoke noisily. *Eee-ooo-sssss-tssss-eeeee!*

"What's that nonsense?" boomed the knight.

"The nonsense that will sink this ship!" cried Kem, tugging on my cloak. "Sparr, we're supposed to be gone by now!"

"Sparr?" cried the knight, lowering his sword. "Sparr! Wait. Who are you?" All of a sudden, he grabbed my special helmet by the horns and pulled it right off my head.

He nearly choked when he looked at me.

I nearly choked when I looked around!

First of all, the giant knight shrank suddenly to a figure only a little taller than me. Second, his massive sword became a gently

curving staff, twinkling with silvery light. Finally, the scene around us was no longer a cargo hold full of bombs and weapons. We were in a bright pink-draped cabin full of bundles and packages.

"Where did all the weapons go?" I asked. "And pink? Why pink?"

"This is Relna's ship," the knight said. "She's a girl and a princess. She likes pink. And we don't have any weapons. This is all food for the hungry people of Nerona!"

Kem tore his helmets off sooner than you could say Goll. "Food? Did you say *food*?"

"Kem, wait. This is some kind of magic," I said. "This knight is tricking us!"

"Oh, you've been tricked, all right," the knight said, holding my helmet up and peering through it, then doing the same with Kem's. "But not by me. Your helmets are charmed. From their eyeholes you see what their owner wants you to see —"

"And hear!" said Kem. "Ko's magical voice is in there, too!"

The knight paused. "I can't believe I've found you. Sparr, do you know who I am?"

"What —"

All of a sudden the orb stopped smoking at our feet and exploded with a boom, hurling us violently across the cabin. The hull cracked and water surged in, sending the heavy cartons of food tumbling and crashing across the floor. I was pinned under a stack of them.

"Kem!" I cried. "Our secret mission! This is not the way it was supposed to happen!"

"No kidding!" he snarled, using both of his heads to chomp his way out of the food bundles he was trapped behind.

Even as flames spread across the room, the floodwaters surged over me. Without a thought, the knight thrust my helmet back on my head and pulled me free of the cartons.

Just in time! The next moment, I heard the terrible snapping of timbers. The hull caved in completely, and we were thrown out into the freezing water.

I tried to swim to the surface, but the flames kept me away. Diving to avoid the sinking hull, I could not find my way in the black water. What I saw instead were the splashing, flapping fins of a mighty sea serpent, darting out from behind a coral reef.

"Ahhhh!" cried Kem. "A sea monster! He's coming right for us!"

The creature's massive pair of fang-filled jaws opened wide.

I couldn't swim away. The beast came so swiftly! Before I could move, its horrible teeth closed over us, and — *snappp!* — we were swallowed!

Five

By Candle Glow

Beffo whirled around from his sizzling soup pot. "A sea serpent . . . attacked you?"

"Yes!" said Kem. "We were sucked down into the darkness of its throat and then —"

"And then," I said, "we sat up and found ourselves on the floor of a Ninn submarine!"

Beffo stared at us for a second, then howled with laughter. "Ha-ha! The Ninns!

They had promised to help you — and they did!"

All five little monkeys squeaked and squealed along with the troll. Still laughing, Beffo spooned out bowls of soup for us while they began stirring the pot again.

And I kept remembering.

Thwunk! Thwunk! Clunk!

I jumped up from the floor of the submarine. The moment I threw off my helmet, I realized that Kem and I weren't the only ones swallowed by the sub.

The Destroyer — or whoever he was — was there, too. In a flash, the Ninns pinned him to a chair and pulled his helmet off. When they stepped away from the chair, I gasped.

"Sparr!" croaked Kem. "He's . . . you!"

He wasn't me, but he looked a lot like me! He was a few years older, but his face was very like mine.

"All right. What sort of trick is this?" I said. "More magic? You stole the voice of Ko from my ears. Now you steal the face my mother gave me?"

He was silent for a long while. Finally, he said, "Your mother gave me this face, too. I'm Galen. . . ."

The name triggered a long-forgotten memory in my mind.

"Galen? Galen . . ." I whispered, trying to remember. "I think my mother told me that name long ago, when I was small. But she was forbidden to say it in the palace. I've never spoken it since . . . since . . . she died."

The boy closed his eyes for a second. When he opened them again, they were wet.

"I guessed that it was so. Sparr, listen. I'm your brother."

I felt my throat swell up and my eyes grow moist. "My brother? My brother!"

I thought about all my lonely years in Ko's palace, not daring to believe I had . . . a family. My thoughts raced, but then, something else began to surface. Anger.

"Brother?" I spat. "So, where have you been all these years? How could you have abandoned me?"

"I didn't!" he said.

"You must have! Or else I would have known more about you. After my mother died, Ko took me in; he cared for me as his own son, as his Prince of Goll!"

"Ko?" said Galen. "Ko is a master of evil and of lies. He didn't care for you! He *kidnapped* you. I've spent the last ten years in Droon looking for you, Sparr!" He stepped closer. "Ko has woven a cloak of lies all around you. Gethwing has, too. I'm no Destroyer, as you called me. Nothing is the way it has seemed to you. You've been under Ko's curse for all these years. You're lingering under his curse now!"

I searched my mind. *No, no, it couldn't be!*

"There's proof. Look," he said, pointing out the vessel's porthole at the city of Nerona.

No longer the shabby black city I had seen through Ko's cursed helmet, Nerona was a glittering vision. Its towers rose high and caught the first rays of dawn from the east, turning its brilliant white stone a shimmering golden color. I couldn't believe the beauty of the city. Nowhere in all of Goll was anything as bright or as beautiful as this.

"Sparr, if you can't believe your eyes, or

your ears, listen to your heart. Deep down, you know it's true. Queen Zara is our mother — *our* mother."

Jamming my eyes shut, I thought of her. I remembered the painting on the wall in her chamber, and that terrible dark figure behind her bed. The look on Ko's face.

He lied to me. For ten years they've all lied to me!

Now my heart told me the truth. I leaped up and embraced my brother. "Galen!" I cried.

"Sparr," he said. "It's been a long time."

"Ahem!" said a voice behind us.

Turning, we saw the Ninn warriors clustered together, their faces bright with candlelight. Among them, they held a cake glowing with candles!

"Family," they said. "Ninns like family!"

Even through our tears, Galen and I laughed as the Ninns began to eat the cake themselves. Kem scrambled around their feet, eagerly catching the falling crumbs.

Finally, my brother wiped his face with the cuff of his cloak. "Sparr, this is amazing. You have to stay with me, of course. Together, we'll find my — our! — older brother, Urik. Maybe return to the Upper World. Or live here in Droon. We'll fight the beasts. We'll do it all together —"

"The beasts?" I said, suddenly remembering Ko's own secret mission. "Galen, the emperor has gone off to the Iron Gate!"

The smile dropped off his face. "The Iron Gate. I've heard of it. It's a half-day's journey from here. What does he plan to do there?"

"He's going to raise the Seven Giants," said Kem. "Big giants. Awful ones, I'm told!"

Galen blinked. "Your dog. Does he speak?"

"All the time," I said. "And I mean, *all*

the time!" Then I snapped my fingers, and when Kem repeated what he had said, everyone could understand him — not just me. Hearing his words, the Ninns grumbled among themselves about the Iron Gate, but still managed to eat more cake.

"Ko wants to battle the Droon army and destroy Nerona," I said. "You've seen his magic. We might never be able to stop him."

Galen smirked. "This is Droon, Sparr. Never say 'never.'" But his expression soon changed to one of fear. "Seven giants, huh?"

"Bigger than big," said Kem. "Humongous! At least that's what the legends say. They're headed by the giant leader. His name is Zor."

Galen stroked his bare chin as if he were scratching a long beard. He kept pacing the small cabin of the submarine, seeming to run something over in his mind. Finally, he stopped. "Nope. There's no time to get help.

We'll have to take on this mission our-selves."

"And do what?" asked Kem.

"Stop the giants. Try to stop Ko. Maybe prevent a huge war," said Galen.

"Are you including me in this?" said Kem. "And will it be dangerous? Answer the second question first!"

Galen laughed. "This is Droon, Kem, so, yes, our mission will be full of danger. And since Sparr's personal friend is a personal friend of mine, you're definitely invited."

Kem nodded both heads. "As long as I don't have to wear any funny armor, I'm in."

My heart was thudding with excite-ment. "Uh, Galen, you said a word before."

"Danger?"

"No."

"War."

"No."

"Friend?"

"Uh-uh."

"Mission?"

"That's it!" I shouted. "It's Kem's and my favorite word!"

"Well, *yours*," said the dog.

"And now we've got at least part of a family, and even maybe some . . . help?" I said, turning to watch the Ninns lick the last of the cake off their six-fingered hands.

The chief of the red warriors grinned a toothy smile. "Ninns have no love for Ko. If Sparr is against Ko, Ninns are against Ko!"

The Ninns raised their hands and all slapped them together. It was a strange moment. I felt that nothing would ever be the same for me again. My heart was pounding, my mind was in a whirlwind. I had just met my long-lost brother. I no longer felt alone in this world. Being with him made me feel like my mother was closer. Even if it meant turning my back on everything I knew, my whole life in Ko's palace for the last ten years, it seemed right. It seemed perfect.

I almost laughed out loud.

In a single night, was I really going from being Goll's youngest prince to . . . an outlaw?

I turned to Galen. The look on his face made me sure. "Ten degrees south, seven degrees east. To the Iron Gate!" I cried.

His eyes twinkling, Galen spun the submarine's wheel. "Full speed ahead!"

Vroooom! The submarine dived deep under the surface and sped toward the east.

Together, Galen and I drove the Ninn vessel deep under the straits of Nerona. Soon the silver water of the Sea of Droon turned black and heavy. Before long, Kem jumped up with a bark. Peering through the submarine's scope, he shouted, "Land ho!"

We surfaced. Beyond the jagged shore

of sharp rocks and crashing waves, we saw a massive wall of black iron.

"Inviting, isn't it?" Galen muttered.

"It gets worse," said Kem. "I just know it gets worse."

The Ninns steered the vessel into a rocky inlet. The top hatch opened, and Galen, Kem, and I climbed out. Cold rain fell from the sky, soaking us instantly. We jumped ashore.

Staring at the giant wall, I felt my heart sink. "A few minutes ago I thought we could do anything. I was full of hope. I was happy. All good things must end, I guess."

"All bad things, too," said Galen. "Especially Ko. Are you ready?"

Taking a deep breath, nervous and scared, but between friends, I took my first step against the emperor. "Ready!"

Six

The Big Black Iron Gate

Even as the three of us crept toward the Iron Gate, shrouded in its terrible shadow, I was amazed at how excited I felt.

"Kem," I whispered. "Two missions in one day? That's pretty good."

"Two missions against two different enemies?" he snorted. "That's better than good. That's a record!"

All of a sudden, Galen halted. He looked up and down the black wall in front of us and sighed. "You know what I figured out? This isn't a gate. Ko may call it a gate, but gates open. This is one solid wall. There's no way through it." He glanced at me. "Do you happen to know any spells?"

I thought back for a minute. "I invented the Foggy Mist of Cloud. It can hide you. Or I could also set fire to your tail, if you had one."

Galen stroked his chin again. "Yeah, I don't know if that's going to help us right now."

"How could Ko pass through something solid, anyway?" asked Kem, running his paws over the sheer wall. "He's not the smallest beast around. Unless there's a door only he can see —"

I gasped. "The magic helmet! Looking through it, I could see through Ko's eyes. Maybe we can see how he got in the gate!"

"Brilliant!" said Galen.

"Your helmet is still in the submarine," said Kem. "I'll get it." He scampered to the Ninn vessel and was back in a few moments.

"Remember when you wear this again," said Galen, helping me on with the helmet, "that I'm not the Destroyer — unless you count all the things I've broken trying to learn our mother's powers!"

I started to laugh because I had done the same thing. But when the helmet fell onto my head, I saw my brother as I had before, a monstrous knight of great size. I began to hear whispering and hissing and knew I would soon be swayed by it. I had to be quick.

Shuddering at the eyeholes' powerful magic, I turned to the black wall and saw it as if through Ko's eyes. Sure enough, I spied a dark, arched opening about ten feet tall and five feet wide.

"I see how he went in," I said. "Come on. And don't worry. It may look like solid wall, but we can go right through."

Pulling Kem and Galen under the open arch with me, I tore off the helmet. I was never so glad to be rid of something in my life. Instantly, I saw what was truly there, and it stunned me. Towering before us was a vast fortress of the same black iron as the outside wall. Even the columns that twisted into the sky were iron, gleaming as if wet with oil.

Soon I heard the sound I had been dreading, an incantation rising from within the fortress.

"*Thugga-nesh! Pitchen-ka-tola!*"

Kem and I shared a look.

"I don't want to be around when Ko finishes his jabbering," he said gravely.

As quietly as possible, we advanced until we came to a large space, open to the sky. We huddled behind a column and looked out to see seven bronze giants, all silent and still, and each over fifty feet tall.

Three of the giants bore large axes. Three others carried lengths of spiked chain. One giant, larger than the others, held both.

Smelling the fumes of his flaming horns and hearing his terrible murmurs, I knew it wouldn't be long before Ko showed himself.

I was right.

Stepping out from amid the forest of columns, Ko howled the final words of his dreadful conjuration. *"Thabash, Zor!"*

No sooner had he said this than a giant foot dragged across the ground and dropped heavily. *Thump!* The earth shook as if it were splitting apart. It nearly sent us tumbling to our knees. The other foot followed with a second earthquaking *thump*!

Before long, all seven giants were alive. Their eyes glowed the color of blood.

Kem grumbled softly, "Oh, this won't be good for us."

"This won't be good for anyone," said Galen, raising his voice. He stepped out from behind the column, and we followed.

When the emperor saw Galen, his eyes flashed in surprise and anger. When he saw me, his horns shot fiery fountains into the air, and he bellowed with rage.

"Sparr? My Prince of Goll? You —*traitor*!" Smoke poured from his nostrils. He gnashed his fangs and beat his chest until the whole iron fortress rang with the sound.

I had never seen him so angry. I didn't know what to do.

"Traitor! Traitor!" he bellowed. "What — have — you — done?"

I fell to my knees. "Ko . . . I . . ."

"He's doing the right thing!" yelled Galen. "Now, you'd better find a place to hide. Your big pals are coming down!"

Without pausing, he twirled his staff and charged fearlessly among the giants, darting between their stomping feet. With blistering speed, he battered them about the legs over and over, like a blacksmith hammering iron.

"Charge!" howled Kem. And he raced into battle, too.

I alone held back, frozen on my knees, unable to move. Whether I was mesmerized by Ko's power or guilty about what I had done, I can't say. But I could not budge from my spot.

Meanwhile, my brother was acting like the warrior I had always wanted to be. As the seven giants swiped at him, he flung his marvelous staff around,

dodging their hacking axes and spinning chains.

Thrusting the tip of his staff between one giant's feet, he yanked hard and sent the bronze warrior wobbling backward into the one behind it. They both thundered to the ground, toppling pillars when they fell.

At this, Ko beat his chest again and breathed black smoke out over the temple. Through the fog his eyes, still blazing like fire, sought me out. In his face was something I'd never seen before.

What was it? Fear?

Was Ko . . . *afraid*?

He took a step toward me.

"Hold on there, Ko!" shouted Galen. "I'm not done yet. Here's one for our mother! Zara, this is for you!" He danced his way between the giants toward the emperor, then sent a powerful blast from the end of his staff. The blast struck one giant in the center of its chest. The beam angled off and struck another, then another, gaining power and speed as it did so. By the time it toppled the sixth giant, it was a bolt of sizzling energy.

Drawing the light instantly back into the staff, Galen aimed it at Ko, then let go with a blinding, thunderous flash of light.

"Sparr! Stop him!" the emperor yelled as Galen's blast streaked through the air. Impulsively, I turned, thrust my sword in the way of the sizzling bolt, took a step to steady myself, and — stumbled over Kem.

"Sparr, you klutz — oowww!" Kem howled.

My sword, catching only a fragment of Galen's fiery bolt, melted in my hands, while — *BAMMM!* — the blast caught Ko full in the forehead.

It hurtled him to the ground with a horrifying cry. "ARRRH!"

Galen had already whirled around toward the last giant. "One more to go!" he cheered.

I shuddered as I drew near the emperor. Black blood flowed from the wound on his forehead. The flames in his horns sputtered.

I felt my heart thunder in my chest. "What have I done?"

Ko stared at me, his face twisted in pain and terror. "Your mother, Sparr . . . you can . . . see her. . . ."

"What!" I gasped. "My mother? She's gone. She's dead! You're lying to me again!"

"Help me, and you will see her!" he said. "Only I know where your mother lies. If I die, no one shall know. But I need your strength!"

I shuddered, not knowing what to do. "No . . . I've found Galen now. . . . I can't . . ."

Suddenly, Ko's gaze fell on the last giant standing, the largest of the seven.

"Zor!" he whispered, speaking the giant's name. "Zor, take him. *Tanak Galensa!*"

Even before the emperor finished uttering his command, the giant sent a sudden beam of fiery light from his red eyes, bursting over Galen and stunning him. Then with a mighty swing of his arm, Zor snatched my brother off the ground, pinning his arms to his sides. He dangled him high in the air.

"Ko!" I cried. "Tell me about my mother!"

"*Zeh-lep-thet,* Zor!" the emperor groaned to the giant. "Kill the wizard!"

"No! Not Galen!" I cried. Before I knew it, I had spun around and uttered a charm I saw my mother use once.

"Solee-bolee!" A sudden shower of frosty light fell over the black fortress. Zor froze. Galen went still in his hand. Kem was stopped in midleap. Only by shielding Ko, did I prevent the charm from affecting him.

The beast ruler swooned in pain, his eyes closing for a moment, then reopening, black and smoldering. "Once again, you disobey my wishes! But you alone can save me now. Bring me to the mountain of Silversnow. It is protected by three strong knights, but you can defeat them. Bring me there now. I am fading . . . !"

"But how? What can I do? I'm just a boy!"

"Take strength from me!" he said. "Come closer . . . closer . . . and I shall give you what I had always hoped. . . ."

He grabbed my hand with a grip like iron. When his terrible claws pierced my skin, my arms tingled as if rivers of power suddenly ran through them.

I felt like the Prince of Goll again. My head swam with strange visions and desires. All at once, my imagination blossomed with the idea of a creature that would drive us relentlessly to the northern plains.

I spoke its name.

"Grompus!" I cried, not knowing where the name came from, but sure that it was right. Before the sound of my word died away, there was a terrible screeching and sliding, as of a heavy mass dragging itself across the earth. Then it came. A giant shaggy worm, thirty feet from snout to tail.

The smell of the creature's fur was heavy and foul, as if it had been lying underground for centuries. It halted in front of me.

With strength I didn't know I had, I dragged Ko up onto the back of the shaggy worm and tied him there with the broken chains left by the toppled giants.

Then I clambered on. "Kem," I said, and the dog was free of the freezing charm I had spoken. He hopped onto the creature's back and clung just behind me, whimpering.

"Sparr, what exactly are we doing?" he asked.

I didn't answer. I didn't know!

One hand gripping my arm again with his dark power, Ko pointed to the north. But before we drove away, I spoke to the giant. "Zor! Set my brother down!"

A deafening, creaking, grinding, and squeaking happened then, and the bronze figure unfroze from my charm's trance. He bowed before my tiny form. I felt so small, cowering beneath him.

"Young master!" he boomed. He set Galen on the ground, still frozen.

As frightened as I was, I found that I

liked — no, I *loved* — the sound of those words.

Young master!

"Go!" I told him. "Return when I say!"

"Your will is my command!" Zor boomed. He stormed off toward the distant hills, leaving his toppled brothers where they lay.

Looking out beyond the fortress, I saw the dark plain purpling in the early dawn. With a flick of my fingers, I took the reins of the Grompus. "North!" I commanded. "To the mountain of Silversnow!"

Kem grumbled sadly behind me, "Oh, Sparr. You and your missions!"

As we left the Iron Gate for the northern plains, my heart was a whirlwind of emotion. Just before the terrible place was out of sight, I turned back and whispered under my breath.

"Galen!"

The charm released him from its power, and Galen began to move.

Whatever else happened was lost in the roar of the wind and the furious spinning of snowflakes as the giant worm drove us swiftly into the north.

Seven

Under the Mountain

The wind howled! Snow came at us from all directions. The air, flashing white under dark skies, was as thick as . . . as . . .

✳

"As troll soup?" interrupted Kem, nearly choking on his bowl.

Beffo laughed suddenly, and a chorus of little chuckles erupted from the monkeys.

"As troll soup!" I agreed, setting my bowl

down and standing closer to the crack-
ling fire.

"But tell me," said the troll. "You knew
Galen would follow you. Why did you
free him?"

I looked at the little creature. "Why
indeed? Time will tell, I think. Time . . . and
the snow."

"Snow?" said Beffo.

"The snow that whirled and whirled
around us, never ceasing for three days and
three nights. Whirling, whirling . . ."

Hour after hour I snapped the leather
reins, and the Grompus slid over the snow,
driving us farther into the land of ice drifts
and frost heaves and storming flakes.

My own mind was storming, too.

Ko's shadow had crept over me again,
but it was weaker than before. Galen had

come into my life, and with him came more and more memories of my mother. But Ko had said we were going to where my mother lay. Even though I knew he had lied to me my whole life, I was in the middle, between him and Galen, my own heart and head spinning, spinning. . . .

I looked down at the stricken emperor. Shivering, strapped to the worm's neck, his glassy eyes were fixed on mine.

Did Ko sense what I already knew? That a little thing, standing firm instead of tripping over Kem, might have saved him? And yet he knew I would go anywhere to see my mother.

Suddenly, I heard the thundering of hooves behind us. "Kem, hold tight. Riders are coming! Grompus, turn!"

"Here we go!" Kem yelped, hanging on for dear life. No sooner had I spoken the words than my wizard brother soared over the snowy ridge behind us, flying atop a majestic, blue-furred pilka. The band of Ninns from the submarine was not far behind him, riding regular white pilkas over the ground.

"Sparr, stop!" shouted Galen. "What are you doing? We've come to help you!"

My heart leaped to see Galen, but I had only wanted him to be free. I didn't want him to stop me.

"Faster!" I cried, whipping the reins of the Grompus and speeding away into the howling winds. Our pursuers were soon lost amid the swirling snows.

And still we drove on, past ruined palaces, coils of smoke pluming from their toppled towers. Once, we passed a fortress aflame after an attack. It was already sinking into the earth, as if the stones were no more than melting blocks of ice.

I shared a look with Kem. "The empire

of Goll is falling around us. Ko held it all together with his power."

Kem nodded. "I'll bet word has already spread that he's been wounded. The beasts were loyal to Ko, but not to one another. They're fighting among themselves now to see who will rule next."

And still we raced northward.

Finally, Ko clutched the worm's fur and pulled himself up. "Worm, halt here!"

The Grompus slid to a stop at the base of a great mountain of jagged rock, its sides thick with snow and glistening ice. Rising from the foot of the mountain to a height of a hundred feet or so was the outline of a giant icy door.

"What's in there?" asked Kem, trembling.

The emperor groaned. "A ship to take us to Queen Zara."

"A ship!" I snarled, feeling he was lying

to me again. "But we're hundreds of miles from the water —"

"An airship!" Ko growled. Then he shuddered. "Hold. The protectors are here. The Knights of Silversnow: Rolf, Lunk, and Smee. Hurry. Our enemy the Destroyer has sent them."

I grew angry at the name. "He's not —"

"To us, he is!" shouted Ko, taking hold of my arm once again. "To our future in Goll — to *your* future — he is the enemy! But look to it! The Knights of Silversnow will try to stop us from entering. Defeat them!"

His voice still commanding me, I leaped down from the Grompus and landed in the snow. Kem jumped next to me. We crept around the side of the mountain as silently as we could.

Not silently enough.

"Hold on there, little one!" boomed a voice deeper than thunder. From what Ko had told me, I knew he was the knights' leader, the one called Rolf. As he stepped into my path, I saw that his bushy-bearded face was squeezed inside a helmet much too tight for it.

There was a movement of air behind me. I spun around to see a second knight, the one called Lunk. I stepped back from him and nearly tripped into a third, who lurched out of the darkness wearing a pair of great spiked gloves. I knew his name, too. It was Smee.

"You'll not stop us!" I growled.

"We shall!" boomed the one named Rolf. "This mountain holds a terrible machine. The beast emperor hid it deep in this rock, but he shall not reach it again. You shall not enter."

"Ko will die if I don't," I told the knight, my hands beginning to feel hot.

Rolf frowned. "Boy, we're not fans of

death, but your evil leader shall not enter here!"

He stood squarely in between the other two knights. Holding his giant shield in front of him, he nearly hypnotized me with the great snowflake spinning around on the front of it. He held a massive, wide-bladed sword at the ready. The other knights stood on either side of him, blocking the silver door.

Since my sword had melted from Galen's blast, I no longer had a weapon. I didn't know what to do.

"I will get by you!" I yelled, sounding braver than I felt. "I will —"

All of a sudden — *blam!* — I was hurled backward into the snow as a blast of red fire shot from my fingertips at the knights. They tumbled into a moaning, groaning heap!

"Grompus, trap them!" I found myself saying, and at once, the worm coiled around

the three knights. It trapped them in its tightening grasp before they could move.

"Boy, inside, now!" boomed Ko, clutching his bleeding forehead. "You know the words that will allow you to enter!"

I *did* know the words, though I didn't know how I knew them. Squeezing my eyes shut, falling deep into my memory, I spoke.

"*Kemah-drakoni-ayra!*"

Once again, a burst of red sparks shot from my fingers. This time, the sparks shattered a waterfall of ice from the face of the stone.

And the door creaked open.

Kem jumped back in fear, both mouths hanging open in amazement. "That's new."

What is this new power? I wondered.

"Inside!" Ko cried again.

I took the massive latch in my hands. With a great pull, I yanked the doors fully open onto darkness. I put my shoulder under one of Ko's arms and helped him in. As soon as we entered the mountain, the doors closed behind us with a boom. We were sealed inside.

"Oh, I don't like it here!" Kem growled.

"What is this place?" I asked.

Ko didn't answer but stared ahead into the darkness. Breathing heavily, he spoke a word.

"Besh-na."

The instant he said it, light showered us.

Walls of ice, nearly as high as the sky, rose up, sheer and frosty and silver all around us. In the center of the icy room stood a large, black-hulled ship. It was the airship Ko had spoken of. It bore the shape of a dragon, with spiked wings curving off the stern. Curling up from the front was a frightening head with fangs bared and twin eyes glowing red.

On either side of the ship, half guarding it, half bowing before it, were six blue beasts like tigers. They were completely still.

"Help me to the deck!" Ko grunted. "And you shall learn the secret of your mother —"

Even before he finished, there came a terrifying sound, and the giant door burst inward. Daggers of ice flew across the room. The knights were back. And this time, still mounted on their pilkas, Galen and the Ninns were with them.

"Sparr!" my brother shouted from his saddle, his eyes wild, his staff shimmering in the silver light. "Don't let him escape. His empire is falling. Don't help him flee!"

I gasped. "Galen . . . I . . ."

Ko's eyes raged. "Only *you* can see her, Sparr! But time is nearly gone! Fly us from here! Fly us!"

Then the emperor bellowed a single

word. *"Ganath!"* The blue tigers that had silently guarded the ship now came to life. They roared and leaped to defend us.

Before I could do anything — *vrrrt!* — a door opened on the opposite side of the cavern. It led back outside into the snows.

As the door slid away, the flat hull of the dragon ship began to move across the icy floor.

Eight

The Air Battle

The moment the tigers set upon the knights, Galen leaped from his pilka to help. He waded into the battle with his staff spinning.

Thwonk! Flang! Thud!

"Ship, fly!" shouted the emperor.

Ko's grip on my arm was like a vise. I couldn't break away. My other hand was on the rudder. I felt myself steering the dragon ship right into the storming snows.

Charging past the tigers, the Ninns hurled ropes over the sides of the ship to hold it back.

"Kem!" I shouted. Without hesitating, he charged from one rope to the other, biting through them. They dangled loosely for a moment, then fell to the frozen ground.

"No!" Galen cried, swinging his staff once more at the blue tigers, sending them howling into the cavern's shadows. "Sparr, do not leave here!"

"Tigers, regroup! Defend us!" I shouted. At once, the blue tigers gathered like a wall between the ship and the attackers. They roared at the top of their lungs, distracting Galen and the attackers, giving the ship time to leave the cavern. The snowstorm outside was a spinning wall of white. Icy wind and flakes surrounded us as the ship lifted into the air.

Up, up we flew, coiling around the

outside of the mountain toward its jagged peak. Kem trembled at my feet as I steered us upward through the icy sky.

"Where did you learn how to drive this thing?" he whimpered.

"I don't know!" I said. It was true, but somehow I *did* know how to do it. Around and around the great mountain we circled until we reached the craggy summit.

"Touch down here!" Ko commanded, and I did. Then, hoisting himself up by the mast, he waved a weak hand at the highest peak and whispered a word.

All at once, the peak shed its covering of ice and there appeared a stairway of black stone, reaching up into the white sky.

"Behold the Dark Stair!" said Ko.

At the very foot of the bottom step, the earth opened up and ice and rocks slid away from a hole six feet long.

I trembled. A glass box sat in the hole.

Inside, almost completely frosted over, lay . . . a body.

"Oh, don't tell me!" said Kem, with a shiver that ran through his entire body.

I trembled as I stumbled from the deck to the ground, and trembled more as I approached the box. When my feet stopped moving, my heart did, too.

Inside the box was the lifeless figure of a woman. She wore a silver crown and silver robes. Her face remained hidden behind a sweep of frosted glass. But I already knew.

My knees gave out from under me. I fell to the ground. "Mother . . . Mother . . . *Mother*!"

With a massive effort, the wounded emperor slid from the ship and drew the box up out of the ground. He laid it on the ship's cold deck.

"Fly us to the Isle of Mists!" Ko growled.

Before I could make a move, I heard

pilka hooves clattering over the snow behind the ship. Whirling around, I saw the great blue pilka and on his back my brother, relentless as ever, his eyes wide with amazement, his staff held high.

"Galen, do not come near us!" I shouted at him. "Ko said only I can see her!"

Without thinking, I sent a blast at the ground near the pilka's hooves. It reared, and Galen fell at the foot of the Dark Stair, tumbling into the hole with a cry.

"Fly us from here!" cried Ko.

I grabbed the rudder with one swift move, and the ship lifted from the summit. But Galen would not stop.

He clambered out of the hole and ran across the summit. Digging his staff into the ice, he vaulted high into the air and grabbed hold of the last Ninn rope still attached to the dragon ship. He swung up and landed on the deck next to me.

Then, turning to Ko, Galen raised his staff over his head. It sizzled with light. "You will fall, Ko!"

The emperor roared. I watched his terrible hands heave open the glass box and paw my mother's folded fingers.

"What are you doing?" I cried.

But Ko pushed me aside. "Away, boy!"

Rising to a great height now, he pointed one hand at Galen. I saw a silvery light flow from my mother's hands into the beast's as if — impossible! — he were drawing some kind of power from her lifeless form!

"This is why I need her!" he bellowed as the clear, silvery light from her hands became in him like filth running through a sewer.

"Lies! Lies!" I screamed. Ko had deceived me again. And I had fallen for it.

My mother's pure magic had become a coil of fiery black air, bursting out the tip of his horns now. It curled up like a snake ready to pounce.

"Zara's magic," he boomed, turning to face Galen, "deathless even in death, gives me great power! Destroyer, suffer the curse that killed your mother!"

"What? No!" I cried.

Why I did what I did then, I have wondered a thousand times, regretted a thousand times, and known a thousand times I would do again!

But I did not think then. I threw myself between Ko and Galen. Before either one could make a move, some instinct took over and . . . I blasted Galen. I blasted him right off the ship. Its ancient railing splintered into a hundred fragments, and Galen tumbled to the snowy summit below.

Then I heard Ko shout, "Sparr! No!"

The moment I began to turn, I felt the blow of his curse on my neck as if I were being attacked by ravaging fangs, as if an arrow, fiery and poisonous, were penetrating my skull.

I fell forward. Black air spun around me like a swarm of crows, shrieking in my ears, until I could no longer hear anything else.

The last thing I saw was Galen thrashing on the ground, his face twisted in a howl of amazement as he stared up at me.

The next moment, I saw nothing but black — black everywhere! — and I collapsed on the deck of the rising dragon ship.

Nine

Monster!

"You collapsed," said Kem, peering out the door of Beffo's hut and sniffing the air. "But you weren't dead."

"No?" I said, feeling so very tired all of a sudden. "I sometimes wonder."

I reached up and ran my fingers over the winglike fins behind my ears. Behind each was the rough scar where it met the skin of my scalp.

"But wait," said the troll suddenly. His little face was rapt with wonder, his mouth hanging open in amazement. "Why did you blast that wizard, Galen? Did you blow him overboard to . . . *save* him?"

I paced the tiny hut, halfway between rage and remorse.

"I . . . I . . . I . . ." I stammered.

But I could not find the words to answer. My mind had already gone back to that moment so many, many years ago.

✱

Whooosh! The dragon ship lifted away from Silversnow, away from Galen lying on the summit and the Ninns and the knights on the ground below.

Coming to, I bolted up from the deck, holding my hands out to steady myself.

"What happened?" I said. "What —"

I stopped. The sound of my voice was different. My words came out in a low rumble. Looking down, I saw Kem backing slowly across the deck away from me, baring his teeth and growling.

"Kem? What's wrong?"

Then — *slishhh!* Out of the corner of my eye I saw a tail, long and thick and covered with scales, slide across the deck behind me. It whipped around my cloak and curled at my feet. I jumped in horror at the sight of it.

And the tail jumped, too!

"What?" I screamed. I turned. The tail turned with me! In my mind, I imagined the tail curving up from the deck to hover above me — and it did!

Its forked tip grazed a forest of spikes that were sticking out of the top of my head. Trembling, I ran my fingers over them, only to find that my head was huge and I had a horrible pair of jagged fins growing up behind my ears.

"What? What! No!" I shouted. "What am I?"

But when I shouted, a sudden lick of flame spilled into the frosty air in front of me. Smoke coiled up after it.

Kem ran and hid, quivering like the puppy he was. First one head then the other peeked over the top of the glass box and gazed at me. "Sparr? What *are* you?"

"Ko!" I cried, feeling sick. "Change me back! Change me back!"

The emperor gasped for air, his own eyes wide in wonderment as he stared at me. Then I saw a faint yet horrible smile flick across his face. Finally, he fell back with a groan, laying his head on the deck. "I cannot, my boy. I am too weak."

My boy? My boy!

I winced at the sound of his words.

"The dragon ship," he said, "will take us to my secret lair. There . . . I shall be healed. . . ."

"*You* will be healed? What about me?" I cried. "How will *I* be healed?"

He did not answer. He said nothing.

I howled at the top of my lungs.

And yet . . . and yet . . . the longer I stayed in this terrible body, the more I felt something else, too. My feet planted themselves sturdily on the deck, their claws biting into the wooden planks. Breathing in the icy air, I felt my chest expand to a massive size. I raised myself to full height and loomed over the stricken emperor. The look on his face was one of pain mingled with a kind of horror.

I was no longer a boy.

I was a monster!

I glanced at my mother. The box had

frosted over again, obscuring the face beneath.

Good! I thought. *If she were alive, she wouldn't even know me!*

Icy wind swirled around me, and I wrapped my cloak tighter around my new form. The dragon ship rose ever higher through the sky.

Standing there, looking down upon the snowy world, with Ko's poison coursing through my veins, I began to assemble pieces of the truth. It came to me then that this curse, intended for Galen, was the same one that killed my mother. Maybe Ko hoped she would become both beast and wizard. Maybe he knew she would never give in. Either way, she died of it. Perhaps Galen would have died of it, too. But I did not die. I lived.

I became this . . . thing.

Why?

Why did I live?

The dragon ship soared south over the wastes of Goll. I despised Ko, hated him, and yet there was something growing in me. A power I had never known.

"Where are we going?" I demanded.

Ko moaned. "To the Isle of Mists. Together with you, the spirit of your mother will heal me! I shall return!"

I stared at the emperor. As my veins went cold with hatred and Ko's dark magic, I felt more powerful than ever.

So was it true?

Was I the most powerful being in Droon now? Was I truly . . . the Prince of Goll?

The snowy land moved below the gliding ship and I roared like a beast. Next to the glass box, Kem trembled. The panting breath of both his heads thawed the frost on the box's surface. Inside lay the lifeless form of my mother, her face as pale as morning.

It was then that I saw something.

Nestled in my mother's pale hands was a small black stone. A memory worked its way to the surface of my mind.

A stone? A *secret* stone?

Was this the secret stone that girl told Gethwing about? Was it?

Gently I opened the box's glass lid and took up the stone. My mother's hands were so cold, yet my own horrible claws tingled when I touched them, and a second explosion, as powerful as Ko's curse, seared my brain. I heard her words in my mind.

Sparr . . . my little love. Take this gift. Someday we will meet in a new home. This stone will help you find me!

Trembling, I held the stone to my chest. *Find you? Where? Your body is here!*

A place of warm sun, and yet of showering snow. Of gentle quiet amid the baying of beasts. Of wondrous trees, yet not of branch or leaf or trunk. I will be waiting, my dearest, littlest boy!

My heart nearly burst then. Even as a horrible beast, a monster on the outside, I was still Zara's son. I knew then what I had to do.

Turning, I wrenched the rudder from Ko's icy grasp and veered off his terrible course.

"No! What are you doing?" he gargled.

But I held my sparking hands over him. "You may have taken me, made me one of you. But you shall never take my mother!"

Against his oaths and raging, I drove the dragon ship to the ground.

We landed on a vast plain of purple earth, somewhere south — far south — of

Silversnow. Pushing Ko away, I lifted my mother out of the box and eased her body from the deck to the ground. Kem, astonished by every action I took, jumped down next to us.

Then, using a charm that came to me in a flash, I sent the dreaded ship up again.

Ko lifted his wounded head over the side and fixed his blood-colored eyes on me. "My beasts will come for you. They will find you!"

"Let them try," I said.

"Now that your mother is dead, there is no magic strong enough to reverse my curse. Whatever you do, wherever you go, you have no choice but to bring me back! You will bring me back — my Son of Darkness!"

Hearing his words, a black pall fell over me. I felt as if I were being ripped apart.

"If I must, I will bring you back!" I yelled,

my head already filled with the image of a snake-shaped crown I would someday make and call the Coiled Viper.

Then, just before the ship disappeared into the clouds, I swallowed my pain and said, "I will bring you back, Ko, when it suits me."

Then the dragon ship — and Ko — soared up and out of sight.

For a day and a night I did not move, could not move. Then I began my journey, dragging my mother's body on a stretcher of branches I made.

As cold as the north was, the plains we crossed were hazy and hot. Two days later, I made out the dark mass of trees in the distance. I recognized it as the Bangledorn Forest. Beasts were forbidden to go inside.

"There," I said. "I will bring my mother there."

✳

The hut was silent for a long while after I stopped talking. The whirling storm outside seemed to calm for a moment. Even the fire's bright crackle seemed to hush in the minutes that followed.

Finally, Kem lifted one head. "That's the way it happened," he said.

Beffo breathed out heavily. The pot bubbled, and he ladled some soup into a bowl and set it on the floor. The monkeys scrambled for it. The troll whistled then, and a little bird flew into the hut. Beffo whispered soft words to the bird, then offered it soup from his ladle. It soon flew away.

"Was that the moment?" asked the troll.

I turned to him. "What moment?"

"The moment you decided to take Droon for yourself?"

Closing my eyes, I thought back to that day. "There was one thing yet to happen."

Kem snuffled. "It happened very quickly."

"It did," I said.

"And I didn't leave, you know," said Kem. "I was there every step of the way. No matter how . . . terrible you looked, you were never really alone. I never strayed."

I petted both of his upturned heads. "No, my friend, you never did."

True, true. Kem was there. He never left my side for an instant as I moved on again, pulling my mother behind me, walking, walking, walking toward the darkness of the trees.

Ten

At Bangledorn's Edge

As we approached the forest, Kem halted in midstep.

"What is it?" I asked.

He sniffed the air. "What Ko said. Beasts would come. Or, actually, one particular beast. I think you know who."

No sooner had Kem said this than we saw a dark blotch in the sky, its four wings flapping swiftly, closing in on us.

I sighed. "It was just a matter of time."

Gethwing landed with a thump. He stomped forward slowly, staring at me.

"You have . . . changed," he said.

"I'm more like you now," I said.

A grin moved horribly across his dragon jaws. "But still an unruly child at heart. You know, I have lived in Ko's horned shadow forever. Today, I saw the dragon ship flying into the clouds. I know he has left us. Now it's my turn. To put it plainly, with Ko gone, I am naming myself emperor."

Kem growled. I said nothing.

The dragon went on, "I have been watching you. You are powerful, Sparr."

I liked hearing that. "Go on."

"Few could do what you have done. I tested you. Ko tested you. *Life* tested you. I dare say carrying your mother's body has tested you the most. Now that you have both the powers of a wizard and those of a beast, you can be a great sorcerer. Under my command, of course."

He paused to glance at my cloak. It was almost as if he was trying to see into its pocket.

"Not long ago, I heard a prophecy. . . ." he began.

I remembered the strange, long-haired girl on the dragon's balcony. "Yes?"

"A girl foresaw the future and predicted your part in it. Now, as Emperor Gethwing, I order you to hand over a certain secret stone that has come into your possession."

I fixed my eyes on the moon dragon. It was my turn to smile.

"Yeah, I don't think so," I said, sounding to my own ears like my brother Galen.

The dragon's expression didn't change, as if he expected me to refuse him. "You think your mother will protect you? Look at her. She is dead. It's only you and me now."

"And me," said Kem. "But mostly you . . ."

At Gethwing's words, my whole body tensed. My tail arched up behind me. Its jagged tip hovered over my head, ready to strike. "You, Gethwing, are not prepared for the power I now have!"

His awful grin vanished and he lunged at me, his claws drawn.

With barely a thought — *tail, strike!* — the ragged tip of my tail whipped out. It struck his neck. He pretended to fall in pain but leaped up suddenly. I tumbled back, and the black stone flew from my cloak to the ground. Its fall sounded like a chorus of bells to my ears.

Then Gethwing called out, *"Sallo-netta-kem!"*

A swarm of wingsnakes dived suddenly from the sky, snapping and clawing at Kem.

My pet cried out in terror. "Sparr!"

It was all I could do to scoop him out of the way. Together the wingsnakes pinned both of us to the ground. Half laughing, half snarling, Gethwing snatched up the stone. He stood over us. "I was wrong about you, Sparr. Your soul is too soft to be a great sorcerer. Risking the power of this stone to save a puny dog!"

"With two heads!" Kem scowled.

"Gethwing —" I raged.

"Yes? Are you going to threaten me now?"

"Soon I'll come into all my powers, Gethwing, and you and I will have a battle. To the death!"

The dragon did not laugh then. He whistled shrilly, and a moment later, he and his force of flying snakes soared away to the south.

"I've lost my mother's stone!" I said.

"But look!" said Kem, pointing.

As I looked into the southern sky, I saw Gethwing and his wingsnakes begin to falter. First one, then another, then all of the beasts plummeted from the sky. One by one they sank through the clouds of the Dark Lands.

I was sure I saw the tiny black stone fall loose from the dragon's claws and vanish, too.

At the same moment, a great loud wind rushed across the plains, then subsided.

"I can't believe it — they're gone!" I cried. "The beasts are gone!"

"That's how that happened, too," said Kem, nudging his bowl across the floor to Beffo's feet. "More, please. What happened was that far away on the Isle of Mists,

Ko had achieved his greatest magic, even without Zara. He conjured himself to sleep. And the beasts —"

"And the beasts," I said, "followed the emperor into his charmed slumber, waiting four centuries for the day when I would raise them all again. For the moment, all the beasts were gone."

"Not quite all," Kem said softly.

I sighed. "No, not quite all."

I stood on the plains looking into the sky, then bowed my head. My horrible head.

Ko was gone. Gethwing was gone. The dreaded beasts were gone. But I remained.

Again I took up my mother's body. We journeyed toward the forest for two more days, then came to a marshy place. Trying to find a way across, Kem and I heard splashing. We turned and saw a girl standing soaking wet among the rushes.

She had dark hair and wild eyes.

I gasped. "I know you!"

"They call me Demither," she said, moving toward me.

"You told Gethwing about the stone!" I said. "He stole it, and now it's lost. How did you know about it? How do you know any of it? The future is all darkness to me."

She stopped a few steps away. "I can't see everything. Only fragments of what is to be, not why or how or if it is good or bad. Gethwing forced me to tell him what I know."

"That stone was a gift from my mother," I said, beginning to cry.

"You'll see it again," she said softly.

I wiped my face on my cloak. "I will?"

Stooping to the marsh, she cupped some

water in her hands. "You are sad," she said. "Here. Wash your face. It will help."

I bowed my head to her cupped hands. The water seemed clear and cold to begin with, but as I splashed it on me, I felt my face burn like fire and my temples thunder in pain.

"What's happening?" I cried.

Moments later, however, I saw my tail — my horrible tail — shrink and disappear behind me. The scaly hide on my arms melted away until only skin remained. Every part of me that resembled a beast vanished away.

I was a boy again, just as I had been!

"This . . . is . . . wonderful!" I said.

"This marsh is fed by a magical spring," she said. "Its water runs all over Droon. I swim in it, even under the ground. It'll refresh you. Remember that, when you return to

that terrible form again!" With that, she sank among the rushes, and the marsh itself disappeared into dry ground, leaving only a small puddle behind.

"Strange girl," said Kem, sniffing at the puddle. "Demither. I wonder if we'll ever see her again."

The water had more than refreshed me. The terrible monster I had been had faded away. I was back to the boy that I was. I whooped with joy, but stopped when I saw Kem staring up at me, not moving.

"What?" I said. "Don't you love it? I'm human again!"

"Eh, not quite human," he said quietly. His four eyes flicked up toward my ears. I reached up.

"Oww!" I pulled down my hand. There was a drop of blood on my finger. Looking at my reflection in the puddle, I saw a pair of fins still growing behind my ears. They were tiny and pale to begin with, but as I watched, they grew darker until they were nearly black.

"So," I said, "are these to remind me that I can never go back? That I will always have the poison of the beast in me?"

Kem had no answer.

In silence I took up my mother's body. In silence we moved toward the forest. I would hide her among its dark trees.

I would hide there, too.

As we approached, the leaves rustled like the soft jangle of chimes, and out filed a host of little creatures. The tallest was three feet from his curl-toed slippers to his wide-brimmed hat. All were dressed in bright-colored robes.

I knew who they were.

"*Droomar,*" I said. "I have come to bury my mother."

"Your mother is welcome, child," said

the tall one. His voice was soft, as if coming from a great distance.

"Child?" I growled, running my fingers gingerly over my fins. "Don't you mean . . . monster?"

"We have watched you for a very long time, Sparr," he said. "Without knowing it, you have brought your mother where she longed to be. Bangledorn Forest is a land of peace, a place without magic."

"I want to live here," I said.

The creature was quiet for a moment, then smiled. "And yet, you know in your heart . . . you cannot. You have a curse upon you."

I stared at him, trembling. My heart sank. The curse of the beast was in me. The poison of dark magic ran in my veins.

He went on, "Do you know what they call your mother?"

"Of course. She's the Queen of Light."

"It follows then," the creature said, "that, even with fins, you cannot be the Son of Darkness! Sparr, we shall honor your mother as no one else could."

I felt so very tired. "But where will I go?"

"Your own way, for now," he said. "The Dark Lands are empty."

I turned to the south. He was right. Ko's beasts were gone. For now.

"The Dark Lands, then."

The ghostly figures took my mother's body lovingly from me and returned to their forest. I did not — I *could* not — turn away from their solemn caravan. Then, at the very edge of the trees, their leader paused. Removing his floppy hat, he fixed his gentle eyes on me.

"There is a legend among the *droomar*. If buried with love, a spirit lives as a tree grows. Its branches grow high in the sky and reach beyond the world of death. In like manner, its roots grow deep into the earth. So deep, they can emerge on the far side of the world!"

Finally, one after another, the *droomar* faded among the trees, until I neither saw nor heard them anymore.

Night came, then the following day. I did not move. I stared into the depths of the forest where I could not go, not daring to follow the little creatures, not daring to leave.

And all the time I cried.

Finally, on the third day, Kem tugged my cloak. "Time to go, master, like the odd little man said. To the Dark Lands. It's our home now. We'll make it comfy. You'll see."

With every step toward the Dark Lands I drew farther from my mother. The darkness of Ko's curse weighed more and more heavily on me.

My chest burned with pain. With longing. With emptiness. I felt hollow. Finally, I felt nothing at all. I could not enter the place where my mother was. Not like this.

On the very edge of the Dark Lands, I raised my fists into the air. "The days of the beasts are over?" I cried. "Then the days of Lord Sparr have come!"

Beffo had stopped stirring the soup and was listening. "The days of Lord Sparr . . ."

Kem sniffed at the hut door. "Yes. He wasn't very nice after that, with Ko's dark power growing in him, year after year. First he united the Ninns. Why they remained loyal, I'll never know. Then he led them in a midnight attack on Nerona, destroying that golden city. He spread the Dark Lands farther west than they had ever been. He made friends with Kahfoo, the serpent. He even enslaved Demither. It was she who, as a child, had tried to free him from Ko's curse!"

"Enough!" I snapped, standing in the hut's doorway. I looked out at the water and saw that the storm had passed. Then I turned and set my eyes upon the misty summit of the island. Finally, I pulled the small stone from the pocket of my cloak.

"I didn't have then what I have now," I said. "Somehow, my brother Galen found this stone, and that wizard boy, Eric, gave it to me. Now my mission — my *real* mission — has begun!"

No sooner had I said this than the island echoed with the sudden sounds of beasts squealing, howling, and baying.

Kem jumped. "The beasts are finally here!"

"We're finally here, too, Kem," I said.

At that, Beffo stood up on his stool, shook the soup from his ladle, and twirled it in the air. Sparks shot from the ends of it, and it lengthened and became a staff.

Eleven

The Tree of Life

I staggered. "But that's . . . that's . . ."

"Galen!" yelped Kem, backing away from the troll. "Galen used to do that —"

The moment Kem said my brother's name, the little old troll began to change. He grew as tall as the ceiling. His pudgy round face lengthened and was draped by a frosty white beard. With a sharp toss, he cast aside his island rags to reveal a cloak of wondrous midnight blue.

"Galen?" I cried. Without thinking, I leaped to embrace him. "Galen!"

"The very same, brother," he affirmed, when we finally pulled apart. "Our mother speaks not only to you, you know! I was drawn to this strange island, too, exactly halfway across the world from our mother's resting place. Forgive my little disguise, but only by remembering your past could you hope to know your future. I believe this is the place you have been seeking all these years!"

The stone tingled in my hand. My mind swam with my mother's words.

A place of warm sun, and yet of showering snow. Of gentle quiet amid the baying of beasts. Of wondrous trees, yet not of branch or leaf or trunk.

I knew it was true. "It is here!"

"Nor have I been idle," said Galen. "That bird from before is none other than Flink, my messenger. The king and queen will soon land with an army larger than you have ever seen. But we are not alone right now, either."

I looked around. "What do you mean?"

He smiled his usual smile. "Friends?"

All at once, the tiny green monkeys began to change — *pop-pop-pop-pop-pop*!

In five seconds, the creatures were not the playful jungle animals they had been. There stood Princess Keeah and the children from the Upper World, Eric, Julie, and Neal, and right there among them, the little spider troll, Max.

"We're here to stop Ko!" said Eric.

"Gethwing, too," said Neal, pulling a gigantic blue genie turban over his brow.

"And whoever else we need to," said Julie.

"Sorry we don't have cake like the Ninns did!" said Keeah.

"Children! Max —" I began.

The low, angry sound of Ko bellowed from the shore. *"Roarrrr!"*

"Yes, well, let's save the touching reunions for later!" said Galen, leaning out the door of the hut, his eyes darting in all directions. His expression was as knowing and intelligent as when we were boys.

My years — centuries! — of being his enemy melted away like snow in the sun.

"Come on, heroes," he said. "Let's be off!"

Heroes? I liked the sound of that!

The moment we left the hut, we heard Ko's war drums thundering, and the splashing and thumping of beasts and serpents on the shore.

"This way to the summit!" chirped Max.

Following their lead, Kem and I rushed through the undergrowth, careful to stay hidden.

"We're very close, boy," I said to Kem. "Our long journey is nearly over."

"I just hope we make it!" he panted.

In a short while, the jungle thinned enough for us to see the massive, seaborne forces of beasts. It stunned me to realize that Ko had mustered such a huge army just for me.

"I guess they really want to find you," said Kem.

"Never fear," said Galen. Then he stopped before a wall of tangled growth. "Well, never say 'never.' But we'll help! Eric, Julie, Keeah, follow the next path to where Zello has moored the *Jaffa Wind*. Lead him to the summit. Max, Neal, double back with me. I have some tricks up my cloak sleeves for Ko. Sparr and Kem, if I'm not mistaken, through these gnarly roots is the way for you! Good luck!"

"Thank you, brother," I said.

It was short and simple, but that's all there was time for. The children and Galen were gone in a flash, and Kem and I pressed farther into the jungle.

High above us stood the peak shrouded in white mist. For once, I knew where I was going. I was being called to go to the island's summit.

No, not to *go* to it.

To *come* to it.

The deeper into the jungle we went, the more words began to fly inside my mind like trapped birds. I pulled the stone from my pocket, and sense formed from the words.

Left up the gorge. Under the black vines. By the path along the chasm.

"This way, Kem!" I said. "My mother is using the stone to tell me which way to go!"

"I'm glad someone is!" he grumbled, running as fast as his legs would carry him.

Watch out for the last rock. It wobbles. . . .

"Whoa!" I leaped clear at the last moment.

"Akkk!" cried Kem, barely jumping off the rock before it slid down the chasm. "You could share some of those words, you know!"

"Ah, yes, sorry!" I said. "Come on. The beasts are getting closer!"

"Didn't we start the day pretty much just like this?" scowled Kem.

"We did! We did!" I laughed, even as I rushed on. We battered through the undergrowth and came to a clearing. Looking down from the height, I saw hordes of beasts spilling up the hillsides below.

No one cared anymore that I no longer had the Viper. I had betrayed Ko. I could not be allowed to live. And Gethwing knew that now that I had the stone again — the secret stone whose power was foretold to him — I would become stronger than him.

Kaww! Kaww! A troop of Gethwing's wingsnakes swooped down from the sky.

"This way!" yelled Kem, tearing a hole through the hedge and dragging me through to the other side. The wingsnakes couldn't follow and flew on.

"You couldn't have done that alone," said Kem. "Good thing we have three heads! One of them is actually thinking. This way!"

We raced all the way to the misty peak, where frost and fog surrounded us. All of a sudden, the stone tingled in my hands.

I grabbed Kem and screeched to a halt.

"What —" he said.

From the earth just below our feet came a thunderous noise.

"This," I said. "This is . . . it!"

Kem whimpered softly, "Oh, dear!"

All of a sudden, the ground burst open

before us, and roots — what I knew were the roots of a tree in the Bangledorn Forest thousands of miles away — exploded up from below. Curling, heaving, grasping like fingers yearning to touch the sky, the roots tore up through the ground, then stopped. But before they stopped, two giant roots parted in the form of an arch.

Between them, we could see a hole in the ground, a vast bottomless pit.

Breathless with wonder and excitement, I turned to Kem. "We're here."

Twelve

All Bad Things . . .

"Pull back to the summit!" I heard Galen yell. Ko's terrible war drums grew louder and more insistent.

Beasts were tearing up through the jungle, getting nearer. Gethwing's wingsnakes circled closer, too.

Standing under the arch of roots, wobbling in a wind rising from the pit below, I couldn't help but close my eyes.

"Oh, not another memory!" I heard Kem

say. "Sparr, shouldn't we think about saving ourselves? Besides, there's no one left to listen but me, and I was there!"

"Not this time," I said. "Not for all of it."

"Sparr, please, they're coming —"

I heard Ko's voice booming, but that was all I heard. My mind was already traveling backward in time . . . back . . . back . . . to the night . . . when it all began.

Back and forth. Back and forth.

I was pacing in a passage deep in the heart of Ko's palace, right outside the very chamber that would soon be forbidden to me.

She was inside.

Queen Zara was in there . . . dying.

Guarding her door was a trio of sniveling, ugly goblins. Kem? There was no

Kem. He came later. And what was I? Five years old?

From inside the chamber came the sound of my mother's coughing. I paused to listen. She coughed, gagged, coughed again, went silent.

"I need to go in," I demanded.

The goblins looked at one another, then grinned coldly.

"Emperor says no," muttered the fattest of the three, a green-skinned creature with pointy ears and arms nearly as long as its legs. I went on pacing before the chamber.

If I was five years old, then for five years, my mother had lingered near death. For five years she had endured the dark, creeping poison in her veins. For five years she had been drawing away from me, even as Ko had drawn nearer.

It would be only hours now. I felt her

final pull away from this life, from me. Soon I would be alone.

But young or not, I was Zara's son. Which meant that I was clever.

"Well," I said to the goblins, "if you won't let me in, I guess I'll just go away."

The goblins laughed. "There's a good boy. Go to your room. Take a sleep. Emperor see you later."

I pretended to go away down the hall. But when I reached the corner, I stole down a narrow passage and, using a chair, climbed to the top of a column. Then I slid sideways into a narrow space between the floors of the palace. Edging along in the tiny space, I was soon looking down between the ceiling stones into my mother's chamber. She was lying in her bed, draped in silken scarves the color of the morning sky. Ko was nowhere to be seen.

Creeping past the chimney stones, I

found a way down from the crawl space and jumped into the room.

"Mother!" I said, running to her bed.

She opened her eyes and tried to sit up, although I could see how it pained her. She smiled and spoke my name. "Sparr, my little prince, my boy!"

I hugged her. Even as I did, I felt the strength leave her again, and she fell back to the pillow. The oily whispering of the goblins outside and the stomping of hoofed feet along the hall told me that Ko was on his way.

"Him!" I said. "I think you would be well if it wasn't for him —"

Even in sickness, my mother's eyes flamed up. "Sparr, be brave and listen. Far from here — so far, I wonder if I shall ever see it again — there is a place of wondrous things. Among them are secret stones, stones full of magic. I gave one to each of your brothers. I had hoped to give one to you, too. . . ."

She paused, coughing and trembling all over. "If there is any magic, any life, left in me, I will see that you get your stone. With the pure good in you, you can fashion your stone into something truly beautiful. Now . . . look!"

She slipped from her bed and stood on the floor, nearly stumbled, but raised her hands overhead as if protecting me from everything.

Even as the chamber door rang with the clumsy sounds of Ko opening it, I saw tiny white flakes, no more than flashes of silver, dart and dance around us. In seconds we were covered with the flakes, her face was wet, dappled with ice and snow, her skin as pale as the midnight moon.

"When you find your stone, here is where

you must go!" She waved her hand, and I began to see . . . black sea . . . and mist on a mountaintop . . . an arch of quivering black roots calling me . . . and snow . . . lots of snow. "I will meet you here —"

There was a sudden noise as the final bolt shot back, and the door squealed open.

The vision vanished when Ko stormed into the room. "Boy! What are you doing here?"

Pushing me gently behind her, my mother twirled suddenly among the flakes, and the air sang with the sound of chimes.

When she thrust her hands at Ko, silver light sprang at him, striking his horns. The beast howled and drew back.

"You will never take my boy!" she said. "You may try, you may curse him as you cursed me! But you will never know the power of light as he does, you dark thing!

He will survive your curse! He will be free of you!"

My mother leaped at Ko again, driving him back to the door with blades of silver light, when the goblins burst in. I rushed at Ko, but he threw me down.

Suddenly, my mother fell to her knees, and I cried out. Looking at me, she breathed her last few breaths. From them a sort of wind rose, and out of that came more snow. Flakes spun in little storms all around the room. Snow fell in the chamber in wonderful flashing designs.

The flakes hissed on the emperor's ashen skin now. He shrieked in pain and squirmed to avoid them. More and more spinning flakes drove him and his howling goblins from her room.

"Son!" she cried suddenly, her voice nearly gone. "You shall never be alone —"

With that, her last breath rushed out, cool and sweet on my neck.

"Mother! Mother!"

The snow still swirling softly around me, I saw something move in the shadows, and a strange creature stepped timidly toward me. It was a puppy. A puppy with two heads.

My eyes swam with hot tears. "She said I wouldn't be alone. Did she . . . send you?"

Both furry heads nodded.

Even in death I knew she would be with me. All mothers love their children, whether they can be with them or not. She would protect me!

The flakes cooled my forehead. They smelled of the piney forest depths and the beauty of the Upper World she had so often told me about.

Hearing Ko in the passage again, I scooped up my dog and fled the room.

*

But now the beasts were crowding toward the island summit in greater numbers than ever. Staring into the pit, I thought I saw a white speck glisten, then vanish in the air. Was it snow? Or were my eyes playing tricks?

Then there came more, flashing here and there in the air around us. Soon flakes were spinning white and silver everywhere.

"Snow," said Kem. "Like in her chamber. I remember, too."

Soon everyone was there, Ko on one side, Gethwing on the other, King Zello, Queen Relna, and my wizard brother and his band of brave heroes taking position behind him.

Looking into the pit, I saw what I had hoped to find. Long, gnarly roots were coiled around the inside the hole, as if the fingers of an enormous tree planted on the far side of the world were reaching up toward me.

I knew for certain what the *droomar* had meant: that "a spirit lives as a tree grows." If this island was exactly opposite the Bangledorn Forest where my mother's tomb lay, then the tree of her spirit had grown through the entire world of Droon and right up to me.

She was calling me.

I turned to Galen and the children and tried to smile. "Four centuries of evil can make quite a mess. I'm so sorry."

Swift currents of snowy air were spinning and rushing among the roots now like silken scarves dancing wildly in the wind.

I turned to my faithful friend. "Kem?"

"*Rooooo!*" he howled. He didn't hesitate, leaping quickly through the arch and into the pit. "Ayeeee!"

The snow swept around Kem and drew him down.

I held the little stone to my heart. With a single leap, I fell, fell, fell into the pit below. As I did, the roots began to twine together above my head, sealing me away from the world.

"Mother, I've found you at last!" I called.

"Sparr!" cried Galen, his voice echoing into the earth after me. "Your fins are . . . gone!"

Finally! I thought. *I am home!*

About the Author

Tony Abbott is the author of more than sixty funny novels for young readers, including the popular *Danger Guys* books and *The Weird Zone* series, as well as *Kringle,* his hardcover novel from Scholastic Press. Since childhood he has been drawn to stories that challenge the imagination, and, like Eric, Julie, and Neal, he often dreamed of finding doors that open to other worlds. Now that he is older—though not quite as old as Galen Longbeard—he believes he may have found some of those doors. They are called books. Tony Abbott was born in Ohio and now lives with his wife and two daughters in Connecticut.

For more information about Tony Abbott and the continuing saga of Droon, visit *www.tonyabbottbooks.com.*